Will Jessica Meet a Movie Star?

"Mrs. Otis," Jessica said, "Daisy Benton will be at the Valley Mall today. Can I ask her to be on our Thanksgiving float?"

"She's the star of *Make-believe Princess,* isn't she?" asked Mrs. Otis.

"Yes! It's the best movie in the world!" Jessica said.

Mrs. Otis smiled. "Of course you can ask her. But I hope you won't be too disappointed if she can't come."

Jessica headed to her seat and smiled at her twin. "Daisy will say yes," she told Elizabeth. "I just *know* it."

Bantam Books in the
SWEET VALLEY KIDS series

SWEET VALLEY KIDS

STAR
OF THE
PARADE

Written by
Molly Mia Stewart

Created by
FRANCINE PASCAL

Illustrated by
Ying-Hwa Hu

BANTAM BOOKS
NEW YORK · TORONTO · LONDON · SYDNEY · AUCKLAND

To Zachary Sekuler

RL 2, 005-008

STAR OF THE PARADE

A Bantam Book / November 1994

*Sweet Valley High® and Sweet Valley Kids are
trademarks of Francine Pascal*

Conceived by Francine Pascal

*Produced by Daniel Weiss Associates, Inc.
33 West 17th Street
New York, NY 10011*

Cover art by Susan Tang

ISBN: 0-553-48111-8

Published simultaneously in the United States and Canada

*Bantam Books are published by Bantam Books, a division of Bantam
Doubleday Dell Publishing Group, Inc. Its trademark, consisting of the
words "Bantam Books" and the portrayal of a rooster, is Registered in U.S.
Patent and Trademark Office and in other countries. Marca Registrada.
Bantam Books, 1540 Broadway, New York, New York 10036.*

PRINTED IN THE UNITED STATES OF AMERICA

OPM   0 9 8 7 6 5 4 3

CHAPTER 1

Princess Jessica

Jessica Wakefield twirled toward the bus stop on Thursday morning. "It is I, Princess Jessica," she announced to an invisible crowd.

Her twin sister Elizabeth giggled. "Tell that to Mom when it's your turn to clear the table."

"Princesses don't do chores, silly," Jessica said. "And I'm a princess. Just like Daisy Benton."

Todd Wilkins and Caroline Pearce, two children from the twins' class at Sweet Valley Elementary School, were already at the bus stop.

"Who's Daisy Benton?" Todd asked, tossing a ball into the air.

"She's the star of the new movie, *Make-believe Princess*," Elizabeth explained. "We saw it at the mall yesterday and—"

"It's Daisy's first role," Jessica cut in excitedly. "And we were at the opening. Daisy plays a girl who wants—"

"Don't say another word," said Caroline, shaking her finger at Jessica. "I'm going to see it this weekend."

Caroline was always telling everybody what to do. Jessica frowned at her. "I was only going to say that Daisy has pretty dark curls," Jessica said.

Caroline covered her ears and began to hum.

"You can see Daisy's curly hair in all the ads, anyway," Elizabeth pointed out as the bus pulled up to the curb.

It made Jessica feel good to know that her sister always stuck up for her. That was one of the things she loved about having an identical twin. But there were a lot of other good things, too.

The Wakefield twins had long blond

hair and blue-green eyes. Even their best friends in Mrs. Otis's second-grade class had a hard time telling them apart. But while they seemed the same on the outside, they were different in a lot of ways. Elizabeth paid attention in class and always did her homework. She enjoyed playing outdoors, especially with the Sweet Valley Soccer League.

Jessica was just the opposite. She never wanted to play outside because she hated getting her clothes messy. Her favorite thing about school was certainly not the work. It was whispering and passing notes to her classmates. But even though the twins were very different, they were still the best of friends.

"If we had a puppy, I'd name her Sukie," Jessica said to Elizabeth. Then, to get back at Caroline for being so snooty, she added, "Just like Daisy's puppy in the movie."

Caroline stopped humming and stamped onto the bus. "No fair. You're ruining the whole movie!" she whined.

The twins' big brother, Steven, got to the bus stop in the nick of time. "Ah, that's a baby movie, anyway. Too bad we didn't see *Monster of Creepy Cove*," he said in a spooky voice.

Now Jessica put her hands over her ears. "Stop it, Steven!"

As they took their seats, Elizabeth looked across the aisle at her brother. "You know Jessica doesn't like scary stories."

"Right. She likes that baby movie." Steven held his nose.

"It is *not* a baby movie!" Jessica protested.

Elizabeth frowned. "I wish you two would stop fighting."

"I thought you were on my side," Jessica whimpered, plunking her book bag onto the floor. "I thought you loved the movie, too!"

"No one could love it as much as you do!" Elizabeth said, smiling.

Jessica sighed. It was true. *It's probably*

the best movie in the whole wide world, she thought. Jessica closed her eyes and dreamed about the day she would be a star just like Daisy.

When they arrived at school, Todd hopped off the bus. "I think we have assembly today," he said.

"That's right," Elizabeth agreed. "Mrs. Otis said we're going to hear about a Thanksgiving surprise."

"Assembly! Yuck!" Steven made a face and ran to meet his fourth-grade friends.

"Well, I think Thanksgiving assembly will be great," Elizabeth said to Jessica. "Don't you, Jess?"

Jessica shrugged. She thought the only good thing about assembly was that she didn't have to do schoolwork.

After Mrs. Otis took attendance, she announced, "OK, class. Time for assembly and our special surprise."

As the class scrambled into line, Elizabeth said to Mrs. Otis, "Can you give us a hint about the surprise?"

5

Mrs. Otis said, "Well, what will most of us do on Thanksgiving Day?"

Winston Egbert piped up. "Stuff ourselves with so much food that we won't even be able to walk!"

"We should all give thanks for a wonderful teacher like you, Mrs. Otis," Caroline chimed in.

"Caroline's always trying to be teacher's pet," Jessica whispered to Elizabeth.

"I was thinking of something that we watch on TV," Mrs. Otis said.

"Football!" Todd called out.

"Parades!" Elizabeth said.

Mrs. Otis smiled.

"Are we are going to have a parade?" Eva Simpson asked. She was one of Elizabeth and Jessica's best friends.

When Mrs. Otis nodded, the class began to clap. Jessica was so excited, she wanted to skip down the hall. *Parades have stars in pretty costumes,* she thought. *Just like Daisy Benton!*

When the children were seated in the

6

auditorium, Mrs. Armstrong, the school principal, came to the front. "I have some happy news, children. Sweet Valley is having a Thanksgiving parade!"

Mrs. Armstrong smiled as the children cheered. Then she continued, "The mall stores and the fire department will have floats. So will the TV and radio stations. And so will our school!"

Jessica and Elizabeth squeezed each other's hands.

"Teachers and parents will help build the float. At lunch, you may sign up for the committee of your choice," Mrs. Armstrong said. "There will be three sections on our float—a tepee, the *Mayflower,* and a Pilgrim village."

Elizabeth looked at her twin. "Let's sign up to build the *Mayflower,* Jess!" she suggested hopefully.

Jessica shuddered. "I don't want to build anything! It sounds too messy."

"Any questions, children?" Mrs. Armstrong asked.

7

Jessica's hand shot up first. "Can we ride on the float?"

"Tomorrow you can put your name into a bowl in the lunchroom. If your name is picked, you'll be on the float."

Jessica began to imagine the fancy costume she would wear. But her daydream was interrupted by Charlie Cashman and Jerry McAllister, the class troublemakers.

"A parade sounds dumb to me," Charlie said in a nasty voice.

"A dumb parade for a bunch of dummies!" Jerry added.

Mrs. Otis turned to the boys and put her finger to her lips. Miss Johnson, a third-grade teacher, went to the piano. "Time for the school song," she said cheerfully.

Jessica's voice rang out as if she were already a star on the float. "Sweet Valley is our joyful school—"

Charlie and Jerry pounded on the seats in front of them and made fun of the song. "Sour Valley is our crummy jail—"

8

This time Mrs. Otis took them to the back of the room.

"Charlie and Jerry are always ruining things for everybody else!" Jessica whispered to Elizabeth.

"Just like you tried to ruin the movie for me!" Caroline piped up from the row behind them.

Before Jessica could answer, Elizabeth tugged on her sleeve. "Quiet, Jess. You don't want to wind up in the back row of assembly!"

Jessica glared at Caroline. *I am not going to wind up in the back row,* she thought. *I, Princess Jessica, am going to be on the float—without Caroline!*

CHAPTER 2

A Trip to the Library

As they got to the cafeteria for lunch, Elizabeth pointed to the sign-up table. "Let's put our names on the *Mayflower* list," she said excitedly to Jessica.

"N-O spells no. I'm a princess. I'm going to *ride* on the float, not *build* it!" Jessica did a fancy ballet pose.

Elizabeth bit her lip. "I know you want to be on the float. But sign up anyway. To keep me company." She grabbed Jessica's hand and pulled her to the line.

After lunch, Mrs. Otis took the class to the school library so they could find books on the first Thanksgiving. "Remember your library manners," Mrs. Otis said at the door.

"No running, no fighting, no loud talking, and we have to treat the books with care," Caroline said. "Right, Mrs. Otis?"

"Is it OK if we breathe?" Winston joked.

Mrs. Otis laughed. "Winston, I know it's hard," she said. "But even you have to zip your lip once we're inside."

Elizabeth, Jessica, and Eva sat at the table under the *Mayflower*-committee sign. Amy Sutton and Ricky Capaldo were already sitting there with Todd, Winston, and Caroline. A class of third-graders was also in the library.

"I'm giving each committee a list of books we thought would be helpful in making the float," Mr. Grasso, the art teacher, announced.

Almost all the children on the *Mayflower* committee copied the names of some books from the list. But Jessica put her head on the table and stared off into space.

11

"Aren't you going to help us find our books?" Todd asked.

"I'm too tired," Jessica replied, rubbing her eyes.

"She thinks she's a princess!" Caroline chimed in.

Jessica giggled. "It is I, Princess Jessica!"

"Princess of Laziness!" Winston teased her.

Elizabeth frowned. She wished Jessica would do some work so the other kids wouldn't say mean things to her. "Each time we find a book, we can bring it to the table. Jess could watch them for us," Elizabeth suggested cheerfully.

"OK," Jessica answered with a big, fake yawn.

The others shrugged and went to find their books.

Elizabeth looked at her list. The first book on it was called *Building Scenery*. She hunted all over the library. Finally she found it on a high shelf. Just as she pulled it down, Bruce Patman, a third-grader, tried to pull it out of her hands.

"That's the one I wanted," Bruce said in a snooty voice. Elizabeth put the book behind her back. "But I had it first!" she said.

Mr. Grasso walked over to them. "Is there a problem, kids?"

Bruce scowled. "My tepee committee needs that book."

"But it was on my list. And we need it for the *Mayflower*," Elizabeth explained, showing Mr. Grasso the book.

Mr. Grasso looked at the shelf. "Uh-oh," he said. "I thought we had two of these. Someone must have put the other one in the wrong place. Maybe we can work out a compromise."

Elizabeth nodded. But Bruce folded his arms. "My father can buy me a million of those books!" he said angrily.

Mr. Grasso shook his head as Bruce walked away. Then he said to Elizabeth, "The very first Thanksgiving wasn't easy. I guess our first Thanksgiving parade won't be so easy either."

13

Especially if Bruce Patman thinks he can boss everyone around, Elizabeth thought. She hugged the book to her as she hurried back to the *Mayflower* table. Six books were piled up in front of Jessica. "These are great!" Elizabeth told her twin.

"Hmm?" Jessica answered. She sounded bored.

Elizabeth shook her head and went off to find more books. But when she returned to the table, she was puzzled. There were no books, and there was no Jessica. She looked up at the *Mayflower*-committee sign to make sure she was at the right table. Just then Winston, Caroline, and Eva rushed over to her, looking very upset.

Winston's face was bright red. "The tepee committee stole our books," he cried. "Jessica was supposed to be watching them!" Caroline pointed to Jessica, who was standing near Mrs. Otis. "There she is!"

Elizabeth rushed over to her twin. Caroline and the others followed.

"One of the books said that England has a royal family. So I think we should have a princess on the float," Jessica was saying to Mrs. Otis.

Mrs. Otis smiled. "But the Pilgrims came to this country to get away from the royal family. The king was mean and wouldn't let them practice their own religion."

"The royal family was too bossy," said Caroline, glaring at Jessica. "And they only cared about themselves!"

Mrs. Otis looked at the unhappy faces of the *Mayflower* group. "Is something wrong, children?"

"Jessica was supposed to be watching our books!" Caroline said angrily. "But she walked away and they stole them!" She pointed to the tepee table.

"It's a free country!" Bruce Patman said with a smirk.

Mrs. Otis thought for moment. "Let's

make a treaty. Just like the Pilgrims and the Native Americans. Each group will get to use the books for two days."

But on the way back to their classroom, the members of the Mayflower group kept giving Jessica nasty looks.

"What a bunch of meanies," Jessica told her sister with a pout. "Well, I'm really mad, too!"

Elizabeth was surprised. "Who are *you* mad at?"

"The Pilgrims! They're the ones who ruined my Thanksgiving. If only they invited the king to come with them, I could have been a princess in the parade."

Elizabeth began to giggle. It was hard to stay angry at her twin for too long.

CHAPTER 3

Jessica's Good Idea

"Let's pretend we're movie stars!" Jessica said to Elizabeth as they cleared the dishes that evening.

Elizabeth shook her head. "I have to look through my library book to find out what we need for our ship."

They went into the den where Mr. Wakefield was reading his newspaper. Steven was watching a game show on TV.

Elizabeth took a book called *How to Build Scenery* from her book bag. "Want to help?" she asked Jessica.

Jessica made a face. "Too boring!" she said.

"No, it isn't," Elizabeth protested. She

pointed to a picture in the book. "This is just like the real *Mayflower*."

Steven groaned. "That whole parade is boring!"

"It is not," the twins said in unison.

Mr. Wakefield looked up from his paper. "What's boring is this arguing," he said.

Jessica slumped onto the sofa and closed her eyes. She smiled, imagining herself riding on the float. When she opened her eyes, she was looking right at a picture of Daisy Benton. Daisy was smiling from the back of Mr. Wakefield's paper. Jessica ran to his chair.

"'Daisy Benton Visits Sweet Valley Mall'!" she read, poking the newspaper. "It says that she'll be at the toy store tomorrow!"

"Funny, that's not what it says on my side," Mr. Wakefield said.

"Dad! There's a whole story about Daisy on this side! Please, can I have it, Dad? Pretty please with sugar on top?"

"Sugar on top?" Mr. Wakefield repeated.

He winked at Mrs. Wakefield as she came into the room. "Now may be a perfect time to make a deal. If I give you this paper, will you clean your bathroom on Saturday?" Mr. Wakefield asked.

"Yes!" Jessica shouted, even though she hated cleaning.

Mr. Wakefield handed the paper to a very happy Jessica. "Maybe I should have asked you to clean the garage too!"

Jessica dashed upstairs. Elizabeth followed her to hear what the article said. Jessica flopped down onto her bed and read aloud. "'Daisy Benton will be at the Valley Mall toy store tomorrow. She will be there to promote *Make-believe Princess*.'"

Elizabeth clapped. "Eva's mom is taking us to the craft store tomorrow for building supplies for the float. Maybe we'll see Daisy then."

"There's no maybe about it," Jessica said. "We *will* see her! And I'll invite her to be on our float!"

"That's a great idea, Jess."

Jessica studied the paper. "Daisy loves playing dress-up and taking dancing lessons. And guess what, Liz? She hates homework and sports. And she even has a koala bear!" Jessica exclaimed. "We're practically twins! We're two peas in a pod!"

"But I have a koala bear, too," Elizabeth said. "And I thought *we* were two peas in a pod."

Jessica glanced up from the paper. Elizabeth looked sad. "We could be three grapes in a bunch," she suggested with a grin.

Elizabeth and Jessica fell back onto their beds and giggled. Then Jessica read the article three more times.

CHAPTER 4

An Unlucky Day

"Look!" Elizabeth cried as they hopped off the bus the next day. She pointed to the sign over the school entrance. "'Win a chance to be on the Thanksgiving float! Put your name in the bowl today in the cafeteria!'" she read.

"Yippee!" shouted Jessica. "I'm going to win. I just know it!"

"That's what *you* think!" said Caroline, skipping past the twins.

In their classroom, Elizabeth followed Jessica to the teacher's desk. Caroline hurried over, too. She pretended to be looking up at the spelling words, but Elizabeth knew she was snooping.

"Mrs. Otis," Jessica began, "Daisy Benton will be at the Valley Mall today. Can I ask her to be on our float?"

"She's the star of *Make-believe Princess*, isn't she?" asked Mrs. Otis.

"Yes! It's the best movie in the whole wide world!" Jessica said.

Mrs. Otis smiled. "Actresses can be very busy. I hope you won't be too disappointed if she can't come."

As Jessica and Elizabeth headed to their seats, Jessica was smiling. "Daisy will say yes," she told Elizabeth. "I just *know* it."

Caroline made a face as she sat down in front of Jessica. "You think Daisy Benton will talk to you? You're lucky if you even get to ride on the float."

Elizabeth cringed as her twin yelled at Caroline.

"Bet a million dollars I *do* ride on that float!" cried Jessica. "And I bet Daisy does too! We're going to be best friends!"

"Settle down, kids," Mrs. Otis broke in. "Work time."

Elizabeth bit on her pencil. She wished Jessica wouldn't brag so much. Especially about things that might not come true.

At lunchtime, the twins waited on line to drop their names into the big bowl. Elizabeth noticed that Jessica was standing with her eyes closed. "What are you doing?" Elizabeth asked.

"Wishing with all my might," Jessica answered.

When it was Jessica's turn, Elizabeth giggled as her sister stood in front of the bowl and whispered, "Please, oh, please!"

"Don't take all day!" Winston called from behind her.

"Lunchtime's nearly over!" Ricky yelled.

"Just a second," Jessica shouted back, squeezing her eyes shut again. She kissed the card with her name on it and dropped it into the bowl. Before anyone could say another word, Elizabeth quickly tossed hers in, too. Then she and Jessica headed for their lunch table. Lila Fowler and Amy Sutton were already sitting there with Eva. Elizabeth sat next to Amy, and Jessica slid onto the bench and closed her eyes.

"Why are your eyes closed?" Lila asked, waving her straw.

"Shh! I'm staying in a lucky mood," Jessica replied.

Amy, Lila, and Eva looked at Jessica and then at each other.

Elizabeth opened Jessica's lunch bag and peeked inside. "Mmm. Cookies. If your eyes are closed, I might eat yours, too," she teased. "That doesn't sound so lucky." Everyone laughed as Jessica quickly grabbed her lunch bag.

That afternoon, Elizabeth stood beside Eva and her mother at the crafts-store counter. Jessica was with them, fidgeting in the doorway, looking out into the mall. "I don't want to miss Daisy," Jessica shouted anxiously.

"We'll be through in a minute," Mrs. Simpson told her. She looked at the list. Then she turned back to the girls. "Where's Jessica?" she asked.

Uh-oh! thought Elizabeth. She and Eva ran to the front door. Jessica was heading for the toy store. "Wait, Jess!" Elizabeth called. "You're supposed to wait for us."

"We have to hurry!" Jessica answered in a worried voice.

Mrs. Simpson took a deep breath. "Remember that you must always stay where I can see you, girls!"

Eva grabbed one of Jessica's hands. Elizabeth took the other and gave it a hard squeeze. She knew how excited Jessica was, but she didn't want her to get into trouble.

A long line of children crowded into the toy store. The mall clown, Mr. Sport-Man, was waving and making funny faces. Elizabeth, Jessica, and Eva stood on tiptoe to see if Daisy was there yet.

"Hey, kids," the clown shouted. "When

I beep my horn, I want everyone to shout, 'Welcome to Sweet Valley, Daisy!'" He honked his horn, and the crowd gave Daisy a Sweet Valley welcome. Jessica's was the loudest of all.

But when Daisy appeared, she was too far away for them to see her. Jessica frowned. "How am I going to ask Daisy to be on the float if I can't even see her?"

Eva smiled. "I know!" she said to Elizabeth. "Let's hold our hands together to make a bridge. Then we can pick Jessica up."

"Good idea!" Elizabeth said. She took Eva's hands and they made a bridge. Jessica climbed on top of them. "Hi, Daisy!" she called.

All the children nearby turned to watch.

"This is going great," Elizabeth whispered to Eva.

"Can you come to our school—" Jessica began.

"Help!" Eva cried. "I can't hold her anymore!"

"You have to!" Elizabeth said.

"Whoa!" Jessica shouted as she began to wobble. She took a step backward to keep her balance and stepped on Elizabeth's hair.

"Ouch!" Elizabeth yelped. She jerked away from Jessica's foot. Jessica took another step and landed on Eva's elbow.

"My funny bone!" Eva cried, starting to giggle. She let go of Elizabeth's hands and rubbed her elbow.

Jessica tumbled to the ground, crushing Elizabeth beneath her. The children standing nearby laughed as the girls struggled to their feet.

"Daisy was looking right at me!" Jessica said excitedly. "Let's try again!"

"Jess," Elizabeth said, "you almost squashed me!"

"Why don't you jump up in the air and ask Daisy?" Eva suggested.

"I would be down on the ground before I could finish," Jessica said.

"You ask a part of the question,"

Elizabeth said. "Then Eva will ask another part, and I'll finish it."

Jessica crouched down low, then jumped as high as she could. "Sweet Valley Elementary School in—" she shouted.

"—vites you to be on our float—" Eva yelled.

"Thanksgiving Day!" Elizabeth finished.

There was no answer. The crowd was busy laughing at Mr. Sport-Man's red nose. "I don't think Daisy could hear us," Elizabeth said.

"Coming through with camera equipment," a loud voice boomed. "We're filming Daisy for the evening news."

Mr. Sport-Man waved a bunch of fake flowers. "Who wants to be on the news with Daisy? Everybody holler 'Macaroni and cheese!'"

"Macaroni and cheese! Macaroni and cheese!" the children yelled. Jessica shouted the loudest.

Elizabeth's heart jumped as Mr. Sport-

Man reached for Jessica. But before Jessica could grab his hand, a man with a microphone pushed between them. "Channel Five News!" he said.

After the man passed, the clown turned and reached for a hand. Elizabeth crossed her fingers. But this time Mr. Sport-Man reached for someone way on the other side of the line. Elizabeth couldn't see whom the clown had picked.

The crowd quieted down as Mr. Sport-Man asked the lucky child, "And what's your name?"

"Caroline Pearce," the voice answered. Then Caroline began to spell her name.

Elizabeth looked at her twin. Jessica's chin was trembling, and Elizabeth was sure that her sister was trying not to cry.

CHAPTER 5

The Ruined Float

All around Jessica, parents, children, and teachers were hard at work on the float. Elizabeth, Eva, Todd, Ricky, and Winston were measuring wood for the sails. Mrs. Wakefield was helping them. Jessica was sitting on the floor of the gym, watching them all work. She didn't want to get too close to the float, because there was sawdust all over the place. Besides, the last thing she wanted to do was help build the Mayflower. She was in a bad mood.

Worst of all, Caroline was prancing around the gym bragging about being on the news with Daisy Benton over the weekend. Just the way she had been bragging at school all day. When Caroline came toward her, Jessica closed her eyes and pretended to be asleep. She didn't want to hear any more about Caroline and Daisy.

Then Jessica heard Mrs. Armstrong greet the *Mayflower* group. "How are all you Pilgrims getting along?"

Jessica opened one eye a little bit. That way she could see Mrs. Armstrong without looking at Caroline.

"Fine," Elizabeth answered the principal. "Want to see our plans?"

"Sure," Mrs. Armstrong said. She looked over the plans. "This is wonderful!" she exclaimed. "You're even making seagull pictures for the background. I'm very proud of you."

"I was on the news on Friday with Daisy Benton," Caroline announced. "Are you proud of me, Mrs. Armstrong?"

Jessica didn't wait to hear Mrs. Armstrong's answer. She got up and ran across the room to where the Native American

34

committee was working on its tent. Bruce Patman looked up at her with a nasty expression. "Our tepee will be a zillion times better than your old ship!" he said.

Jessica glared at Bruce. But before she could answer him, she noticed Andy Franklin and Kisho Murasaki huddled near the Pilgrim-village part of the float, looking very upset.

"What's wrong, guys?" Jessica asked.

"Look what somebody did!" Kisho said, pointing at the Pilgrim cabin.

"Oh, no!" Jessica cried. Someone had scribbled all over the cabin door.

"I'll bet Bruce Patman did it!" Andy said. His face was bright red. "He's always saying his committee is the best. And he's so dumb he can't even spell 'Pilgrims'!"

Jessica looked again. The writing said: *Dummy Pillgrums*. And the *s* was backward.

"I'll get Mrs. Armstrong!" Jessica said, running over to the principal.

Andy began to cry as he showed Mrs. Armstrong the ruined cabin.

Mrs. Armstrong shook her head. "I'm so sorry, kids," she said sadly. "Let's get Mr. Grasso. I'm sure he can help."

As the boys walked away with Mrs. Armstrong, Jessica saw Caroline coming toward her. She ducked behind the Pilgrim cabin to hide. On the floor next to the cabin was a book with brightly colored pages. Jessica sat down and began to look at the pictures. One showed a beautiful girl with long braids. Under the picture it said, "Pocahontas: A Native American Princess."

Jessica's heart raced. *I've got to find Mrs. Otis!* she thought. She spotted Mrs. Otis at the water fountain and ran to her.

"If I get to ride on the float, can I be this princess?" Jessica asked, holding up the picture. "Please!" she added.

Mrs. Otis laughed. "I think that would be lovely."

"Yippee!" Jessica shouted. She wanted to tell Elizabeth right away. But before she could find her sister, Lila and Ellen came running up to her.

"Guess what?" Lila said in an annoyed whisper. "We just heard on the radio that Daisy Benton will be at the pet store tomorrow. Caroline's bragging about seeing her again."

"She says she and Daisy are best friends," Ellen added.

Jessica swallowed hard. She wasn't going to let Caroline get to her! "Well, I'm going to see Daisy tomorrow and invite her to be on our float," Jessica told her friends. "And I'll be on the float, too. I'll be a Native American princess. So I'd better practice." Jessica climbed on top of the float and began to wave to her imaginary fans.

"Jessica, look out!" Winston called. "You're standing too close to the sail!"

"Yeah, be careful—we worked all night to get it perfect," Todd yelled.

Lila stamped her foot. "And quit showing off, Jessica! You don't even know if you're going to be on the float!"

But Jessica ignored them all. She knew she was meant to be on this float. She blew kisses to the make-believe crowd and twirled around. "What did you say, fans?" she sang. "You want my autograph? No pushing, please. Everyone will get my autograph in a minute!"

Jessica spun around until she got dizzy and tripped. She heard a crunching sound as she fell into the *Mayflower*'s mast. The wooden frame broke into little pieces! Jessica jumped away so quickly that she tripped again. This time she fell against the cotton sail. Everyone gasped when they heard a loud tearing noise.

"We worked on those sails all night!" Caroline whined.

"How are we ever going to fix it on time?" Todd groaned.

"Thanksgiving is three days away!" Amy added.

"Oops," said Jessica.

CHAPTER 6

Another Unlucky Day

On Tuesday Mrs. Otis's class took turns talking about Thanksgiving.

Elizabeth went first. "I read that the Native Americans taught the Pilgrims how to plant corn. They put little dead fish near each seed. The fish were used for fertilizer."

"Yuck!" Winston yelled, grabbing his throat. "I used to love corn!"

The whole class laughed. "And the Native Americans and the settlers promised to help each other," Elizabeth continued. "For fifty years they lived in peace."

Todd went next. "When the Pilgrims got here, they didn't have time to build each family its own house. So they built one big house and all the Pilgrims lived in it," he said. "But one day it burned down, and they had to start all over again."

"Just like somebody broke our ship!" Winston said loudly.

"And now we have to start all over again!" Ricky groaned.

Caroline frowned at Jessica. "We'll never be able to fix it in time for the parade," she said.

"Who cares about the dumb parade, anyway?" Charlie yelled out.

Mrs. Otis clapped her hands for quiet. "Settle down, children," she called.

Elizabeth looked over at her twin. Jessica's cheeks were pink. She knew Jessica felt bad about breaking the sails. But Jessica hadn't done it on purpose—not like the person who scribbled all over the Pilgrim village.

Jessica waved her hand in the air, and Mrs. Otis called on her. "Today Daisy Benton will be at the pet store," Jessica said brightly. "And I'm going to read Daisy this letter."

Jessica took the letter out of her pocket. "Dear Daisy. I hope you can be on our Sweet Valley Elementary Thanksgiving float. I know you're a busy movie star, so I won't be mad at you if you can't come." Jessica glanced at Caroline. Then she continued reading. "You and I have a lot in common. I love to wear pretty clothes and play with my dolls. We're almost like twins."

Elizabeth was upset. Why did Jessica want to be Daisy's twin when she already had a twin sister?

Caroline's hand shot up. When Mrs. Otis called on her, Caroline said, "Maybe *I* should invite Daisy to our float. We're almost best friends, you know."

"Jessica has already volunteered," Mrs. Otis said. Then she announced that it was time for recess.

As the class lined up to go outside, Mrs. Otis turned to Elizabeth. "Today's the day Mrs. Armstrong gets our attendance sheets. Would you and Jessica take them to her office?" she asked.

41

Elizabeth took Jessica's hand, and they headed for the principal's office. "Let's hurry!" Jessica said. "I don't want to miss any of recess."

After Elizabeth handed the attendance sheets to Mrs. Armstrong's secretary, she and Jessica walked as quickly as they could toward the playground. All the other kids in their class were supposed to be outside for recess, so Elizabeth was surprised when she saw Charlie and Jerry come running out of the gym. The boys looked surprised to see Jessica and Elizabeth, too.

"What were you doing in the gym?" Elizabeth asked them.

"We were just looking at your ugly *Mayflower* float," Charlie said.

"Yeah! It's going to be the worst float in the whole dumb parade," Jerry added. Then he and Charlie laughed and ran down the hall toward the doors.

"What's the matter with them?" asked Jessica angrily.

"I don't know," Elizabeth said with a

frown. "They want to ruin Thanksgiving for everyone."

"Look!" Elizabeth said. She and Jessica were walking toward the pet store with their mother. "Daisy's up front already."

This time, Daisy was standing on a table at the front of the store so all the children could see her.

"Daisy's dark curls are so beautiful!" Jessica exclaimed. Elizabeth laughed as Jessica tried to twist her hair into curls. They kept popping out.

"Hi, kids," Daisy said into the microphone. The pet-shop owner put a little puppy into her arms. "This puppy looks just like Sukie in the movie, doesn't she?" Daisy asked.

"Yes! Hi, Sukie!" the children shouted.

"This crowd is even bigger than yesterday's!" Jessica told Elizabeth in a nervous voice. "Now we'll never get near her!"

"Who wants Daisy's autograph?" a voice called out.

Elizabeth looked at the mall clown. Mr. Sport-Man was collecting autograph books for Daisy to sign.

"Give me your letter to Daisy," Elizabeth said.

Jessica handed it to her, and Elizabeth tugged on the clown's sleeve. "Mr. Sport-Man, could you give this to Daisy?"

"One honk means yes," the clown answered. He tweaked his big nose. It honked once. "My, my! This must be your lucky day!" Mr. Sport-Man said as he took the note to Daisy.

A girl holding a bunch of balloons stepped in front of Elizabeth. "I can't see!" Elizabeth said. "What's happening?"

"Mr. Sport-Man just put my note down on the table in front of Daisy!" Jessica squealed with delight

"I'm so excited, Jess," Elizabeth exclaimed.

"Me, too!" Jessica said, smiling from ear to ear. "Oh, Liz! She's reaching for it! Daisy's reaching for the note!"

Elizabeth stretched up on her toes and tried to see Daisy. But the balloons were too big. "I'll bet she'll say yes!" Elizabeth said, grinning. "I'm so proud of you, Jess!"

"Me, too! Me, too!" Jessica answered, jumping up and down. "Daisy's looking right at my note!"

"She'll ride on our float! I just know it!" Elizabeth said. "Cross your fingers, Liz! She's holding the note."

"Yippee!" Elizabeth crossed her fingers.

"Oh, no!" Suddenly, Jessica's eyes grew wide with horror. "This isn't real. Maybe I'm having a nightmare!"

"What's wrong?" Elizabeth asked, holding her breath.

"Sukie," Jessica gasped. "Liz, the puppy just ate my note!"

CHAPTER 7

A Thanksgiving Lesson

That night, while everyone worked on the float, Jessica sat on the floor in the hall outside the gym. She planned to stay there until it was time to go home. If she didn't go into the gym, nobody could tease her about what had happened to her note. Thanksgiving was only two days away, and she still hadn't reached Daisy. Maybe I should just give up, Jessica thought sadly.

Suddenly the gym door opened and Elizabeth ran into the hall. She looked upset. "Jess! Somebody broke the *Mayflower* sail again, and they scribbled all over the tepee!"

Jessica gasped. She got up and ran into the gym with Elizabeth. All three groups were shouting at each other.

"You guys ruined our tepee because it was better than your junky ship!" Bruce Patman yelled. "My father will sue you!"

"We did not," Todd screamed back. "I bet you smashed our ship after we worked so hard to fix it up again."

As the grown-ups tried to calm the kids, Jessica got an idea. She pulled her twin aside. "Remember how Charlie and Jerry came out of the gym today at recess?" she asked. "And the nasty things they said about the parade?"

"That's right, Jess!" Liz exclaimed. "Do you think they did this?"

"I'll bet they did!" Jessica said. "Let's tell Mrs. Otis."

"But we don't have any proof," Elizabeth called as she followed Jessica.

Mrs. Otis listened with a serious face as Jessica and Elizabeth told her about Jerry and Charlie coming out of the gym.

"Thank you, girls," Mrs. Otis said when they were finished. "But I can't really do anything without more proof."

"That's what I thought," Elizabeth said, shaking her head.

Mrs. Otis stared at the scribbling for a moment. Then she said, "But I have an idea how we could get proof!"

Mrs. Otis called Jerry and Charlie over to the side of the gym. Jessica sneaked over to see if she could hear what they were saying. Then she ran back to Elizabeth.

"Mrs. Otis asked Charlie to write the word 'Pilgrims' on a piece of paper," Jessica said. "And he spelled it just like that." She pointed to the scribble on the tepee. It said, "Dummy Pillgrums."

"He even made the s backward!" Jessica continued. "Then Mrs. Otis told them she thought it was odd that he spelled that word the same wrong way."

"Then what happened?" asked Elizabeth.

"They admitted that they did it!" Jessica said triumphantly.

"I can't believe they would be so mean," Elizabeth said. The girls watched as Mrs. Otis marched the boys over to Mrs. Armstrong. The principal's face got red, and she wagged her finger at Charlie and Jerry. Then Mrs. Otis took the boys out of the gym. Jessica was sure she was going to call their parents.

Mrs. Armstrong blew her whistle. "Children!" she called. "I know you're all very angry. But I want you to settle down now."

"What are we going to do?" Lois Waller cried.

Lois sometimes got teased because she cried a lot. But today nobody said a word to her. Everyone else felt like crying, too.

Suddenly Jessica had an idea. She raised her hand. "Mrs. Armstrong? You know how the Native Americans and the Pilgrims taught each other things? Well, the tepee committee really knows how to

51

make things with papier-mâché. And the Pilgrims are good painters. My Mom can make new plans very fast, and all the committees can help each other."

Mrs. Armstrong looked at Mrs. Wakefield. "How do you feel about doing a new set of plans, Mrs. Wakefield?"

Mrs. Wakefield was beaming as she looked from Jessica to Mrs. Armstrong. "I would love to."

For the rest of the night, everyone worked their best to get the float fixed. Later, as they were getting ready to leave, Mrs. Armstrong called out, "Thanks to all of you for working so hard. I just know that we're going to be finished in time. And now we're going to pick the names to see who gets to ride on the float."

Jessica crossed her fingers as the room grew quiet. Mrs. Armstrong began to call the winning names. "Andy Franklin, Amy Sutton, Bruce Patman, Caroline Pearce . . ." And the very last name to be called was "Elizabeth Wakefield."

On the ride home, Jessica slumped against the backseat. Tears filled her eyes.

Elizabeth leaned over and grabbed Jessica's hand. "Are you sad because I won?" Elizabeth asked in a soft voice.

Jessica shook her head. "I'm sad because *Caroline* won and I didn't," she sniffled. "I'm sad because Daisy isn't coming to the parade. I'm sad because—"

Elizabeth held her ticket out to Jessica. "Here, Jess. You want this ticket more than I do. And no one will know the difference, anyway."

"Thanks, Liz!" Jessica cried happily, bouncing up and down in her seat. She took the ticket and kissed it. "You're the best sister in the whole world!" she cried. "I just *knew* I'd get a winning ticket if I wished hard enough!"

CHAPTER 8

A Lucky Surprise

After school on Wednesday, Mrs. Wakefield took the twins to the doctor's office for their checkup. As they sat in the waiting room, Elizabeth read a book and Jessica put high heels on her Sassy Sabrina doll.

Suddenly, the front door opened and a girl with short red hair limped in.

"Ow! My foot!" she cried as her mother helped her to a chair.

"I'm sorry, dear," the mother said with a worried look.

Mrs. Wakefield leaned toward the other woman. "Why don't you go ahead of us since your daughter is hurt? We're just here for a checkup."

"That's so nice of you," the woman answered.

Elizabeth smiled at the injured girl. "Want to read a book?" she asked.

The girl shook her head and kept on crying.

"Maybe she'd like to hold your Sassy Sabrina," Elizabeth whispered to Jessica. "That might make her feel better."

Jessica's sigh told Elizabeth that her twin didn't feel like sharing. But Elizabeth was glad when Jessica brought the doll to the girl.

"How did you hurt yourself?" Jessica asked.

"Jumping on the bed. I fell off," the girl sniffled.

"Were you trying to fly?" Elizabeth asked in a serious tone. The girl shook her head. Then she smiled and nodded yes.

"My sister fell out of a tree once," Jessica said.

"Did you get hurt?" the girl asked Elizabeth.

"I broke my arm," Elizabeth said. "But now it's good as new!"

The girl looked from Elizabeth to Jessica. "You're twins!" she cried.

Elizabeth stared at Jessica. Then she turned back to the red-haired girl. "So that's why she looks so much like me!"

Jessica stared at Elizabeth. Then she looked at the girl and said, "Twins! And I just thought she was being a copycat!" The three girls burst into laughter.

"I'm getting hungry," the girl said to her mother.

"We'll go to Lee's restaurant tonight," her mother said.

The girl wrinkled her nose. "Another restaurant? Yuck!"

Jessica's eyes grew wide. "Yuck to *restaurants*?" she asked.

"You'd hate them too if you ate out for two weeks straight," the girl said sadly. She rocked the Sassy Sabrina doll. "I've got an idea. If you're visiting from out of town, how about having dinner with us?" Mrs. Wakefield suggested.

The woman looked at the three girls. "They *are* having fun together," she said. "Are you sure it's no trouble?"

"No trouble at all," Mrs. Wakefield said.

The three girls clapped and shouted, "Yippee!"

Just then the doctor poked his head into the hall. "Hi, Mrs. Wakefield. Would it be OK if Mrs. Benton comes in before you and the twins? I think Daisy might have sprained her ankle." Jessica's eyes lit up. "*You're* Daisy Benton?" she gasped.

Elizabeth gazed at Daisy's straight red hair. "But what happened to your long dark curls?"

"That was a wig, silly!" Daisy chuckled. "For the movie."

CHAPTER 9

Daisy's Visit

Daisy sat between Jessica and Elizabeth at the dinner table. "It's so nice of you to have us here," Mrs. Benton said.

"I'm happy you were able to come," Mrs. Wakefield replied. "And I'm delighted that the doctor said Daisy's ankle will be better soon." She helped Daisy to some salad.

"Isn't it fun to sleep in a hotel?" Jessica asked as she passed Daisy a glass of milk.

"It gets boring," Daisy said.

Jessica could hardly believe her ears. "But you don't have to go to school every day. And you get to wear such pretty clothes."

"I still have homework," Daisy said. "And that wig *itches*!"

Everybody laughed.

"Steven," Mr. Wakefield said, "please pass Daisy the rolls."

"Since they're rolls, how about if I roll them down?"

"Roll them down!" Daisy repeated, exploding into laughter.

Daisy actually thought Steven was funny! Jessica looked at Elizabeth and shrugged. She knew Elizabeth couldn't believe it either.

Mr. Wakefield handed the bowl of stew to Mrs. Benton. "How do you find Sweet Valley, Mrs. Benton?" he asked.

Mrs. Benton smiled. "It's such a pretty town. I love it."

"Want to know how I find Sweet Valley?" Steven asked.

"Yup," Daisy replied. "How do you find Sweet Valley?"

"I just open the front door, and there it is!"

Daisy laughed so hard, she almost fell off her chair. "That's the funniest thing I ever heard!" she cried.

The praise made Steven act even sillier. He filled his cheeks with big chunks of potato. "Look! I'm Mr. Potato—"

Mr. Wakefield shot him a look, and Steven quieted down. But all through dinner, Daisy laughed at everything Steven said.

After supper, the three girls went up to the twins' room. "I love being at your house," Daisy said. "And Steven is so funny. It must be great to have a big brother."

Elizabeth and Jessica exchanged baffled looks.

"Let's play dress-up," Jessica suggested.

"Let's dress up like three twins!" Daisy exclaimed.

They pulled the box of dress-up clothes from the closet and dug through it. Jessica found three huge scarves. "We can wrap these around us and pretend they're fancy dresses," she suggested.

When they had finished wrapping the scarves around themselves, Daisy ran back to the box. "What's this?" she asked, tugging at some yellow yarn under a big pocketbook.

Elizabeth helped her pull it out. "It's leftover wool that our mother braided together." She plopped it onto Daisy's head. "Now you have a blond wig if you ever need it for a movie."

Daisy swung her head back and forth. "It's too loose," she said.

Jessica got a barrette and fastened it in Daisy's blond wig. When she was done, Daisy looked at the twins and smiled.

"Let's braid your hair, too!" she suggested with a twinkle in her eye.

Jessica braided Elizabeth's hair. And at the same time, Daisy braided Jessica's hair. Then the girls ran to the mirror and stared at themselves.

"You know what?" Daisy asked.

"What?" the twins answered together.

"I think we look like so much alike, we could all be triplets!"

"We're three grapes in a bunch," Jessica said, grinning at Elizabeth. She knew Elizabeth felt bad because Jessica had wanted to be Daisy's twin. But that didn't mean Jessica ever wanted to stop being Elizabeth's twin.

"Now I have two twin sisters!" Daisy said happily. Then she spotted the koala bear on Jessica's bed. "Hello, koala!" she cried, giving it a hug. "I've got one just like this!" she told the twins.

"Me, too!" Elizabeth held up her koala bear.

"Me, three!" Jessica giggled, flopping down onto her bed. "Guess what, Daisy? We read about your koala bear in the paper."

"And we came to see you at the mall twice," Elizabeth said. "But it was too crowded to get very close."

"At the pet shop, I even passed you a note, but the puppy ate it," Jessica said.

"I remember that!" Daisy laughed. She took a shiny bracelet from the dress-up box and put it on Jessica's wrist. "Anyway, I'm glad we got to be friends now, aren't you?" she asked. "And we're really, really all twins, right?"

Jessica and Elizabeth nodded happily. Jessica took a deep breath and looked at Elizabeth. She crossed her fingers behind her back. "The note was to invite you to our Thanksgiving parade. I wanted to ask you to ride on our school float."

"Sure I will, my twinnie," Daisy said, grinning at Jessica. "We twins have to stick together!" She took a green floppy hat from the dress-up box and put it on Elizabeth's head. "Well, my other twinnie," she said to Elizabeth, "what would I be in the parade?"

"You could be a Pilgrim or a Native American princess—anything you want," Elizabeth explained. She ran to her desk and got a book of Thanksgiving pictures for Daisy to see.

Daisy flipped through the pages. "I know!" she said, pointing to a picture of a Pilgrim family at dinner. "I love those big hats. I can be a Pilgrim wife. And Steven should be my Pilgrim husband!"

Jessica twisted her braids nervously.

"Steven doesn't have a ticket," she explained.

"But he might be able to get one," Elizabeth said.

Jessica's stomach did a flip-flop. She knew that Elizabeth was thinking about Jessica's ticket. *It was Liz's ticket first, and she was very nice to give it to me,* Jessica thought. *But I wanted it more than Elizabeth did. And now it's mine!*

"But even if he *got* a ticket, Steven wouldn't want to ride on the float," Jessica argued quickly. She really wanted Daisy to be on the float so that everyone would see that Jessica and Daisy were friends. But how would people know they were friends if Daisy was riding next to *Steven?*

"Maybe we can talk him into it," Elizabeth said eagerly. Jessica looked from Daisy's hopeful face to Elizabeth's grinning one.

"OK," Jessica said weakly.

CHAPTER 10

Thanksgiving Day

Elizabeth and Jessica went down the hall to Steven's room. He was gluing the wings on a model airplane.

Elizabeth took a deep breath. Getting Steven to ride on the float wasn't going to be easy. She looked at Jessica for support, but Jessica was staring at the floor.

"Daisy will ride on our Thanksgiving float, and she wants you to ride on it, too," Elizabeth blurted out in one quick breath.

Steven shuddered. "Me on the float? No way." He pretended to fly his plane in the air.

Jessica wore an ear-to-ear grin as she

headed for the hall. Elizabeth ran after her. "Wait, Jess. I think we should try harder. What if Daisy won't ride on the float without him?"

Jessica bit her lip. "Life isn't fair!" she groaned. They went back into Steven's room.

"Would you be on the float if we did your chores for a week?" Elizabeth bargained.

"Nope," Steven said.

"What if we did them for two weeks?" Elizabeth pleaded. She knew how important it was to Jessica that Daisy be in the parade. Steven just had to agree!

Steven gazed at the ceiling. "Three weeks," he said.

"Two weeks is our final offer!" Jessica piped up. Steven shook his head. "Three weeks or no deal."

"OK," Elizabeth said. Just then, Daisy's voice rang out from downstairs.

"Guess what, Mom? I'm going to ride on the Thanksgiving float. And Steven's going to be my Pilgrim husband!"

"What?" Steven exclaimed, his eyes wide with horror. "Daisy's Pilgrim husband! The deal is off."

"Please," Elizabeth begged. "She already told her mother."

Steven folded his arms. "No!"

"How about if we do your chores for one month?"

"Oh, no!" gasped Jessica.

Steven shook his head. "Two months."

"Five weeks," Elizabeth said.

"Six weeks," Steven said.

"OK," Elizabeth agreed. She grabbed Jessica's hand and pulled her out of Steven's room before he could change his mind. "We did it, Jess!" she cried. "Isn't that great?"

"Giving up my ticket *and* doing Steven's chores for six weeks? I don't think that's so great!" Jessica sniffled sadly.

Early on Thanksgiving morning, the Wakefields and Mrs. Benton took the twins, Daisy, and Steven to see the floats

69

before the parade. The TV station's float was a giant screen showing dancing turkeys. The fire department had an old-fashioned fire engine, complete with a dalmatian riding on the back.

Elizabeth was thrilled as the music of the high-school marching band filled the air. Everyone was getting ready for the big parade. She smiled at Jessica. But Jessica looked sad. Elizabeth knew her twin was still wishing she could ride on the float.

Steven looked almost as glum as Jessica. His eyes were fixed on the ground, and he kept pulling his Pilgrim hat farther down on his head. *He hopes none of his friends recognize him,* thought Elizabeth.

When they reached the school float, Mr. Grasso greeted them all. Then he turned to Daisy. "Well, little Miss Benton," he said, "on behalf of Sweet Valley, I don't know how we can thank you for riding on our float!"

Daisy's face lit up. "I know how you can thank me."

"How?" Mr. Grasso asked.

"Let Jessica and Elizabeth ride on the float with me!"

"Yippee!" cried Jessica. Elizabeth hoped Mr. Grasso would say yes.

The art teacher smiled. "Let's see what we can do." He turned and called over his shoulder. "Do we have some extra costumes in the trunk, Miss Johnson?"

"How would you like to be a Native American princess?" Miss Johnson asked Jessica. She showed Jessica the costume.

Jessica jumped up and down. "Look, Liz, it's exactly like the one in the book! That's just what I was wishing for!"

"I will take that as a very happy yes," Miss Johnson said. "And for you, I have a Pilgrim costume," she told Elizabeth.

After the girls put on their costumes, Mr. Grasso showed them where to stand on the float. Elizabeth frowned when she saw that Jessica was supposed to stand right beside Caroline Pearce. Caroline was dressed as a Native American princess, too.

"I'd like you and Caroline to hold hands

when our float goes out onto Main Street," Mr. Grasso told Jessica.

Elizabeth bit her lip as Jessica and Caroline looked away from each other and rolled their eyes. She hoped Jessica would be nice to their neighbor, but she had a feeling that Jessica would rather be the only princess on the float.

Suddenly Daisy laughed. "I know you!" she said happily. "You're my friend Caroline, aren't you? We were on the news together, remember?"

Caroline gulped, "I remember, Daisy."

"You know Jessica and Elizabeth, too?" Daisy asked.

"We live near each other," Caroline answered uncertainly. "And we're in the same class."

"Yippee!" Daisy shouted. "My three best friends in Sweet Valley are all in the same class. Caroline and my twins!"

Elizabeth breathed a sigh of relief as Jessica and Caroline giggled and slowly reached for each other's hands.

MAYFLOWER

People lined up along the streets. Children sat on the curb. Parents held toddlers on their shoulders. The drums began to pound as the floats rolled down the street.

"Here comes the Sweet Valley Elementary School float," the parade announcer boomed as the *Mayflower* passed the reviewing stand. "It's absolutely beautiful. The young Pilgrim bride is Hollywood's newest star, Daisy Benton. The young man beside her is Sweet Valley's latest star, Steven Wakefield!"

Elizabeth smiled to herself as she saw a big grin cover Steven's face. *After all the fuss he made about hating the parade, he's actually enjoying it!* Elizabeth thought.

Elizabeth called to Jessica. "Our brother is Sweet Valley's latest star! Maybe he'll give us his autograph."

Jessica laughed. "This is the best Thanksgiving ever!"

SIGN UP FOR THE SWEET VALLEY HIGH® FAN CLUB!

Hey, girls! Get all the gossip on Sweet Valley High's® most popular teenagers when you join our fantastic Fan Club! As a member, you'll get all of this really cool stuff:

- Membership Card with your own personal Fan Club ID number
- A Sweet Valley High® Secret Treasure Box
- Sweet Valley High® Stationery
- Official Fan Club Pencil (for secret note writing!)
- Three Bookmarks
- A "Members Only" Door Hanger
- Two Skeins of J. & P. Coats® Embroidery Floss with flower barrette instruction leaflet
- Two editions of *The Oracle* newsletter
- Plus exclusive Sweet Valley High® product offers, special savings, contests, and much more!

Be the first to find out what Jessica & Elizabeth Wakefield are up to by joining the Sweet Valley High® Fan Club for the one-year membership fee of only $6.25 each for U.S. residents, $8.25 for Canadian residents (U.S. currency). Includes shipping & handling.

Send a check or money order (do not send cash) made payable to "Sweet Valley High® Fan Club" along with this form to:

SWEET VALLEY HIGH® FAN CLUB, BOX 3919-B, SCHAUMBURG, IL 60168-3919

NAME_____
(Please print clearly)

ADDRESS_____

CITY_____ STATE _____ ZIP_____
(Required)

AGE_____ BIRTHDAY_____ /_____ /_____

Watch for

That's right! Your favorite twins, Jessica and Elizabeth, are coming to TV and right into your living room each and every week!

Share all the fun and excitement of their high school romances, friendships and intrigues with each new, must-see episode!

Check your TV listings for day and time. And don't miss any of the great Sweet Valley High books—available at your local bookstore!

Bantam Doubleday Dell
Books For Young Readers